CW00853346

Four Tails

An Anthology of Four Tales for Children

Christine Harris

authorHOUSE®

AuthorHouse™ UK Ltd.
500 Avebury Boulevard
Central Milton Keynes, MK9 2BE
www.authorhouse.co.uk
Phone: 08001974150

First published by AuthorHouse 10/04/2011

ISBN: 978-1-4520-7643-0 (sc)

This book is printed on acid-free paper.

George and the

'Welsh' Dragon

Chapter 1

George saw the moving shape on top of the mountain and shouted 'It's a dragon!'

William said, 'That's rubbish!'

Mum said, 'That's nice dear.'

Dad said, 'Humph!'

George said nothing. He knew it was a dragon. He just knew! He looked at the heavy lidded eyes staring at him, the scale covered body, spiked tail and grasping claws creeping towards him. George gasped!

He looked at Dad.

He looked at Mum.

He looked at William.

He was the only one who could see the dragon.

The creature walked with giant strides, his bulging eyes watching them from outside the car window. His flaring nostrils belched out green smoke as they moved in and out, up and down.

'Wow!' thought George. 'I **like** him.'

George smiled and the dragon smiled back with his shiny, luminous eyes blinking slowly. From that moment on, George and the dragon knew they were going to be firm friends. When George arrived at his grandmother's house, the dragon had wrapped himself around the edge of a nearby lake. His tail dipped in the water and his head was lying on his front claws as he lay at the base of a high mountain.

After lots of hugs and kisses from Mamgu, his grandmother, supper and a last peep at the dragon George climbed into bed. He had a fluttery feeling in his tummy, a fluttery feeling that told George that there was an adventure about to begin.

The next day Mum, Dad and William were off shopping. George didn't want to go.

'I'm going hunting for dragons,' explained George.

William smirked. 'Watch they don't eat **you** for supper, little bro.'

The family left through the front door and George ran excitedly outside to the back garden. The back garden was steep and rose steadily to an old, wooden gate. This, in turn opened up to the mountainside. George could hear the hum of the bees and the bleat of the sheep as he wandered over the hilly landscape. George jumped over the sheep droppings (bobby currants Mamgu called them) and walked through the buttercups and clover towards the lake. There was his dragon waiting for him.

With a swish of his tail and four giant steps forward, the dragon was soon sitting next to George. The dragon looked at George. His down turned mouth gave him a very sad look and George knew that his new friend was not a very happy dragon.

'Do you know what people in this village like best?' asked the dragon. George shook his head.

'Dragons,' answered the scaly creature with a great, big sigh.

'That's good, isn't it?' added George. 'You're a dragon so I'm sure they'll like you.'

'No!' answered the dragon. They like furry ones, plastic ones, dragons on key rings, dragons on slate coasters, mugs, hats, all sorts of things but no one is interested in a real dragon. They like dragons but not dragons like me. It's not much fun when there's no-one to talk to and everyone pretends you're not there.' The dragon told his tale in a deep, husky voice and swallowed hard as a lump came into his throat. George had to swallow hard too. 'Perhaps you need to be introduced to the people in the village' he suggested. 'Mamgu says everyone should be introduced.' George took a deep breath.

'By the way my name is George.'

The dragon shuddered.

'Don't worry, just George,' laughed George.

The dragon flared his nostrils sending out fast, scarlet flames with purple and green smoke. 'You'll have to control that habit if you want to meet new people and make friends,' warned George.

'At least until they know you better. Come on, let's go.'

Chapter 2

The dragon and the little boy ran down the side of the mountain to the village. Mr Jones shouted across to George.

'Good morning! Nice to see you back with us!' He did not see the dragon.

'Hello George. Holiday time again is it? I hope the weather stays fine for you,' smiled Mrs Thomas. She did not see the dragon. Mr Williams gave George a wave. He did not wave at the dragon.

'What about my dragon?' George quietly whispered to himself.

'He's invisible,' added a voice behind George. He turned around quickly to face a tall figure dressed in a gold and blue patterned cloak, a pointed hat and a scarlet star- covered robe. He had a long white beard and held a white staff in his hand. Round his waist hung a thick, metal chain encrusted with jewels of many colours.

'Hello. Let me introduce myself,' smiled the wizard.

'I am Merlin. Merlin Jones to be precise. Don't go confusing me with the 'other one' will you? I'd like to think I'm related but I don't know for sure. Mam always said there was a chance.

Anyway, I'm here to help. You know, if the people were able to see your dragon, they would be afraid. People are always afraid of things that they don't understand. He would be in great danger,' explained the wizard.

'But he needs some friends,' complained George. 'He's lonely.'

Merlin nodded in agreement. George suddenly felt very brave.

'Merlin, could you help him? People are afraid of big dogs too. But everyone loves a puppy.'

'I don't think a marvellous dragon like this should be changed into a puppy,' added the wizard. George shook his head.

'No, but you could change him into a baby dragon.' pleaded George.

Merlin's eyes twinkled at George's excellent idea.

'Caradoc,' ordered the wizard. 'You are about to shrink!' George watched, his eyes open wide.

'Caradoc! So that was his name,' thought George to himself.

'Caradoc was the name of a Welsh prince who lived a long time ago,' explained Merlin as if he could read George's thoughts. 'He deserves a grand name if he's the only dragon left in Wales, don't you think?'

'A grand name; just like yours!' grinned George.

Merlin nodded, winked and murmured some very strange Welsh words.

'Wow!' exclaimed George as the dragon shrunk to the size of a sheep. 'Will he grow again?'

Merlin smiled. 'Oh yes. He will grow to his true size again, but slowly, so that people will get used to him. Old Mrs Jenkins from number 15 walked past on her way to Mrs Morgan's for morning coffee. She peered at George over her spectacles and then down at Caradoc.

'He's a fine dragon if ever I saw one. It's about time we had a real dragon in Wales.' George looked up at Merlin and grinned. The wizard and George just had to agree.

'Very tidy, I must say,' added Dai, the postman, as he passed with his bundle of letters. 'Wait until everyone sees you!'

It didn't take long for the people of the village to meet Caradoc. News travelled fast in a small village and soon there was quite a gathering outside Mrs Williams' shop.

'Very good for business, that dragon. I've never had so many customers in one morning before.'

George introduced Caradoc to Gareth next door and very soon Gareth had brought all the children of the village to see the dragon. They were delighted but a little nervous as they approached the green scaly creature with his long, pointed tail wrapped around George's legs. Caradoc was also nervous and a little shy of meeting everybody. The children giggled and patted him on the head. A little girl called Chloe stood some distance away watching with interest. She clutched a picture she had painted of a red dragon. She smiled shyly as George beckoned for her to come closer. She held her picture, still dripping with wet paint, and handed it to Caradoc.

'It's for you,' she said. Suddenly George realised something. He whispered to Gareth.

'A Welsh dragon should really be red, shouldn't he? But ours is green. Do you think anyone will mind?'

Gareth shrugged his shoulders. 'I don't,' he grinned.

Chapter 3

Mamgu was quite delighted to have an extra guest to stay, albeit an unusual one. She made up a bed for Caradoc in George's room. She lined an old tin bath with lots of thick, woollen shawls and put it next to an electric heater so that the dragon wouldn't get cold.

'I only have one rule,' she warned. 'No breathing fire in the bedroom!'

George's mum and dad were pleased that he had a new pet. William didn't believe in dragons. He didn't want to know.

That night as George lay in his bed he could hear Caradoc telling Mamgu tales of long ago when Welsh princes ruled in large castles and the air was filled with magic and mystery. 'Just like today,' thought George. He could hear Mamgu telling the dragon about the castle in Blodynmelyn.

'It's in ruins now, but the tourists like to come and see it. There's a princess lives nearby. They like to come to see her too. We're probably the only village in Wales which can boast a real castle, a real princess and now a real dragon.'

George pulled the duvet up further and snuggled down into the warm bed.

'I'll take Caradoc to see the castle tomorrow,' thought George. 'He'll enjoy that.'

And so, after a long tiring day of befriending dragons, George fell fast asleep.

'Who's the princess?' George asked Mamgu the next morning.

'Princess Poker Face, we call her,' grinned Mamgu. 'She never smiles and never bothers much with the villagers. She parades around the place and shows up at garden fetes and launches new boats. She's always on the front pages of the newspaper. She likes the attention. Always posing for the cameras but the tourists love her.'

Mamgu rolled her eyes in disgust.

'They've come for years to see the castle, as you know, but now with a new princess to match, they can't keep away. Tourists and reporters everywhere! It used to be lovely and quiet here.'

George couldn't help thinking that Caradoc wasn't going to make it any quieter.

After breakfast, Gareth called with some friends and they and George climbed the mountain that led to the old, ruined castle. Caradoc came too, as guest of honour. He was enjoying all the attention and loved every minute he spent with the children. They played hide and seek, and wrestling dragons. They made buttercup and daisy chains to hang round the dragon's neck. Caradoc balanced a ball on the end of his nose and chased the children round the castle. A dragon in Wales was great fun and the people in the village of Blodynmelyn were soon feeling very happy about it all.

Nothing so good and special as a real dragon can stay secret very long and soon news of Caradoc left the village and spread into the towns. Important looking people arrived with their briefcases to discuss matters of importance. People with microphones, cameras and notebooks sat and watched the mountains for signs of the dragon that lived in the village of Blodynmelyn.

The visitors who had once come for a glimpse of Princess Poker Face weren't interested in her anymore. All they wanted was the chance to see a real Welsh dragon. They brought their cameras and waited; patiently. Mr Sheblee, the manager of the only hotel in the village, 'The Royal Albert,' had a busy time looking after the many people who came to stay. Bed and breakfast places put their signs 'Sorry, no vacancies' in the windows.

Chapter 4

Princess Poker Face, who usually had lots of attention, was not pleased. Heads no longer turned as she passed by. A dragon had replaced her and she didn't like it. Each morning the headlines in the newspaper mentioned the dragon in Wales and each morning Princess Poker Face became less and less amused.

'That dragon is a nuisance,' she squealed one morning. 'He has got to go!'

Next day Caradoc was sent an invitation in the post. He was to go and visit the princess in her home at the end of the village.

Mamgu had noticed the royal crest on the envelope. She said nothing but she worried about it all day. George was out for the day with William and his parents. They had left early to catch a train up to the top of Snowdon, the highest mountain in Wales. George had wanted to take Caradoc but Mum laughed. She thought it was best not to take a dragon on to the mountain railway.

'It gets very crowded and I'm sure people won't want to squash up on a seat with a spiky dragon.'

Despite missing his new friend's company, George had a wonderful day. He took some good photographs of the views from the summit of the mountain. He bought a t-shirt from the souvenir shop and a cap for Caradoc with the words 'I climbed Snowdon the hard way' printed on the front.

When George arrived back at Mamgu's house he ran straight up the stairs to tell Caradoc all about it. The dragon wasn't there. George was worried. Mamgu told George about his invitation and said that she was worried too. William said that he'd probably flown away and wasn't coming back. George poked his tongue out at his brother.

'He'll come back,' reassured Mum as she tucked George into bed. George wasn't sure.

The next morning Caradoc still hadn't returned.

'He is a dragon after all,' said his mum. 'I'm sure he can look after himself.' George nodded but he wasn't too sure. He knew that Caradoc, even with his spikes and fire-breathing tricks, was really, deep inside, as gentle as a kitten. If he was in danger George knew that he was too small to protect himself.

George gobbled up his cornflakes and slurped his juice at top speed.

'I'm going out to play, see you later,' called George. He grabbed Mamgu's rolling pin and metal tray which was propped up behind the biscuit barrel. Perhaps the picture of the red dragon in the centre of the tray had made him feel brave. Whatever he was thinking, as he ran out of the house he looked just like a real knight ready for battle.

He slammed the door behind him and jumped down the front garden steps two at a time. George looked along the street and saw a news reporter standing at the bus stop. He was jumping from one foot to the other as if waiting for a bus that was obviously late.

'Have you seen any sign of Caradoc this morning?' asked George as calmly as he could, trying to hide the tray and rolling pin behind his back.

'No,' answered the reporter, 'but that Princess what's-er-name told us that he was going on a little trip.'

'No he isn't,' answered George. 'That's not true!'

'She said he wouldn't be back for a long time,' argued the reporter. 'I'm just off to the docks to wave him off, take some pictures and so on. Nice touch that would make in tomorrow's Journal.'

'Dragon's Farewell!'

'Princess waves goodbye to her dragon!'

The reporter could see that George was upset. The number 22 bus pulled up at that moment and George jumped on. The reporter paid both their fares as George hadn't brought any money. His only thought was Caradoc and the fact that he was in great danger.

Chapter 5

The half hour journey seemed to take forever but eventually they arrived at the docks to see Princess Poker Face at the centre of the action. She was enjoying the attention of newspaper reporters and camera crews taking her photograph.

'This way your highness,' they called.

'Lovely shot!'

'And another!'

She didn't see George.

George noticed that the princess was now glancing nervously towards a large, wooden crate sitting on the deck of a small boat, its label clearly marked EXPORT.

'Caradoc!' thought George. 'He's in the crate!' George jumped up onto the top of the crate. He waved his rolling pin in the air to attract everyone's attention.

'Quick,' he shouted. 'The princess is late; help her up everyone!'

Princess Poker Face had no time to object for, in seconds, four reporters grabbed her by her arms and legs and lifted her onto the boat. Once she began to protest, no one could hear for all the cheering. The captain of the boat led her swiftly to a small cabin, pushed her in gently and closed the door. He turned a key in the lock and on the door he pasted a label marked 'FOR EXPORT.' He winked at George.

'We can't export a Welsh dragon from Wales, can we George?' grinned the captain. George recognised the voice and the wink at once.

'Merlin!'

The old wizard put his fingers to his lips.

'Shh, it's our secret. I tell you something; you make a fine knight my boy. A very brave one and a very, very good friend. Your courage and friendship was stronger than any of my magic. You have just saved a dragon for Wales!'

George smiled a big, beaming smile as the crate was opened and Caradoc, tired but none the worse for wear, climbed out. George couldn't believe his eyes.

'Caradoc, you're red! A red dragon!'

Merlin chuckled. 'Well, I couldn't resist a little dabble of magic. When I heard of what was happening-well, I saw red, as they say-and this happened. Wales will love him!'

And so they did. Caradoc's fame spread even further. George, happy knowing that his friend was no longer lonely, continued to enjoy the rest of his holiday with his family. Meanwhile, with Caradoc's fame growing, both the dragon and the villagers began to dislike the many visitors who came to search for a dragon in Wales. The village wasn't the peaceful place it used to be. Worst of all, Caradoc remained in hiding more and more and the villagers missed him. At last, Mr Sheblee, who couldn't cope with his hotel overflowing every week, told the television news people that it had all been a great, big joke.

'What silly people,' he said. 'Do you really believe in dragons?'

The film crews and reporters blushed with embarrassment. The tourists smiled and added that they had only come for the peace and quiet. They all packed up their dragon mugs, red, furry dragons and slate coasters and left. It was also time for George to leave. He went to say goodbye to Caradoc. They met on the side of the mountain; in the same spot they had introduced themselves, weeks before. George's eyes were full of tears as he hugged his dragon friend tightly.

'I'll miss you,' he whispered to Caradoc. The dragon looked sad and George knew that his scaly friend was going to miss him too. A large tear rolled out of Caradoc's shining eyes and settled on the end of his flaring nostrils.

'I'll miss you so very much,' sniffed George, 'but I'll be back.'

Caradoc nodded. He was a Welsh dragon living in Wales; he was where he belonged but he knew that he wasn't anything without his special friend. So George went home and Blodynmelyn settled down to quieter times. Princess Poker Face, it was said, travelled in her boat to a far off country, married a handsome prince and lived happily ever after, which is just how stories go. And Caradoc? Well, even though he missed George every day, he really did decide that peace and quiet was what he liked best. He sits, as he has always done, watching over the village. He visits his friends, in the village, every year, before the holiday season, and everyone says,

'How tall you've grown!'

Wales really does have a dragon, a dragon that has many friends and many secrets. He gazes towards the distant hills and waits for a little boy. And somewhere in England, a little boy thinks about him often and looks forward to his next visit to Wales. When George does arrive at the little village of Blodynmelyn, Caradoc greets his special friend in the same way as he always did. He walks with giant strides towards George, watching him from outside the car window. His flaring nostrils belch out red smoke these days but as soon as George sees him he grins and shouts 'It's Caradoc!'

William says 'That's rubbish!'

Mum says 'That's nice dear.'

And Dad says 'Humph!'

Squeak!

One cold, damp morning a little mouse ventured out of a hole in the wall of an old, ruined castle. She sat down on her hind legs, wrapped her long tail around her tummy and sobbed. Mole, tunnelling underground, heard her crying.

'Oh dear, dear little mouse what's the matter with you today?' asked Mole as he came rushing along, squinting in the sunshine.

'I've lost ma squeak!' answered the mouse sniffing little sniffs with her tiny, pink nose.

'Lost your squeak? Well I'll be glad to help you find it. Tell me something about it. Perhaps you could tell me what your squeak sounds like?'

'Oh it's very, very loud. You can hear ma squeak for miles and miles around when it starts,' whispered the mouse.

'Oh don't worry. I think I know where your squeak is.'

Mole disappeared into the bushes and returned with Rabbit who was carrying a very big set of bagpipes. Mole blew into the mouthpiece and made a great big squeak! Mouse put her hands over her ears.

'Och no! Ma squeak is loud but no' that loud.'

Mole explained to Rabbit that Mouse had lost her squeak.

'I am trying to help her find it.'

'Well, if your squeak is anything like the bagpipes your squeak is obviously loud,' said Rabbit. 'Can you tell me? If I touched it, how would it feel? Would it be spiky or slimy?'

'Och, no,' Mouse sighed. 'Ma squeak feels soft and furry.'

'Ah,' replied Rabbit, 'I think I know where it is. I was hopping past the main gateway last night when I tripped over something lying on the path. It was very dark but I am sure it felt very soft under my feet. Do you think it could have been your squeak?'

Mouse looked up anxiously.

'Oh, let's go and see. Ma poor squeak could be hurt.'

Mouse, Rabbit and Mole ran along the hedgerow until they reached the gateway of the old castle.

'Here it is, here it is,' called Rabbit. 'It's still here.'

Mouse looked at the flat, furry pouch lying on the stony path and cried out,

'That's no ma squeak! That's a sporran!'

A shuffling, scraping sound told them that the sporran was not empty. Rabbit lifted the flap and Mole looked inside. A small, shivering vole blinked as the light shone in to disturb his sleep.

'Hello, I was just sheltering from the cold. I must have fallen asleep.'

'Have you seen a squeak?' asked Mole,' because Mouse seems to have lost one.'

Vole pondered a little. 'Well, I don't know if it was a squeak but I did hear something rustling in the breeze this morning. It didn't sound very loud.'

'Was it furry?' they all asked.

'Well, yes, I'd say it was a little furry.'

'What colour is your squeak?' asked Vole gently as he wiped a tear away from Mouse's cheek. 'Is it purple by any chance?'

'Och it is, it is,' gasped Mouse. 'Ma squeak is loud and furry *and* purple.'

Mouse, Rabbit, Mole and Vole were now very excited.

'I'll lead the way,' said Vole. 'Follow me.'

The small group of animals crawled under the hedge and into the meadow beyond. On the very edge of the meadow a clump of thistles were blowing in the wind and making a tapping and a scraping sound against the fence. Some of the flowers had died and in their place was a mass of furry seeds just waiting to blow into the air.

'They're not loud,' said Rabbit.

'No, but they are furry!' said Mole, balancing on the stalks to feel them between his padded claws.

Vole looked at the few flowers that were still blooming.

'They're a nice shade of purple,' he said apologetically.

Mouse shook her head, sat down and once again sobbed into her hands.

Four earwigs, known to the locals as forky- tailies, came scuttling by. They stopped when they saw the small group of puzzled animals standing by the hedgerow trying to comfort a very sad looking mouse.

'She's lost her squeak,' explained Rabbit, 'and we're trying to help.'

'It's loud and furry,' added Mole.

'And purple,' joined in Vole.

'Can you tell us something else about your squeak?' asked the first forky- tailie, trying to help.

'Does your squeak have a smell? We're very good at smells,' said the second forky- tailie.

'Ma squeak smells of rose water and sweet tea,' answered Mouse.

'Yuck!' whispered Mole.

Rabbit frowned at him. Mouse gave a small, timid smile for the first time that morning.

'We smelled that smell yesterday,' said the third forky - tailie. 'Come with me and we'll show you lots of smells like that.'

'But I only have one squeak!'

Rabbit put a comforting paw on Mouse's shoulder.

'Never mind. Your squeak may be there. Let's go and see.'

So, Rabbit, Mole, and Vole pushed Mouse along as they followed the four forky - tailies towards the smells of sweet tea and rosewater. Mouse kept insisting that these smells couldn't possibly be her squeak.

'There is only one squeak in the whole wide world,' she said, over and over again.

It was quite a walk but eventually the little troop marched through tall, wrought iron gates and into the most beautiful rose garden they had ever seen. Everyone sniffed loudly.

'Achoo!' sneezed Mole as the smells of the roses floated into his nostrils.

'What a delight,' murmured Rabbit.

'Sweet tea and rosewater,' cheered Vole.

'Are these your squeaks?' asked all four forky – tailies at once.

'I only have one squeak. These are nothing like my squeak, except for the smell.'

'Hello there,' called all four forky - tailies at once, looking up towards a nearby rose bush. 'We're looking for something.'

A fifth forky - tailie popped his head out of a rose bush.

'Can you help us? We're looking for a squeak; it belongs to Mouse.'

'Tell me about your squeak. I've finished my lunch so perhaps I could help you in your search.'

'My squeak,' said the mouse, sniffing between her tears, 'is loud, furry, purple and sweet smelling and it is as shiny and bright as a sparkling jewel. Oh I miss my squeak so much.'

'Got it!' said the new forky - tailie, crawling out from beneath the petals of the dazzling orange-yellow rose.

'I know where your squeak is. But it is lying in a very dangerous place.'

Mouse cried out with fear.

'Oh ma poor squeak. Please help me to save ma squeak.'

All the creatures looked at each other with a frown.

They didn't feel very brave. They didn't mind helping to look for a squeak, but to go on an adventure and face terrible dangers was not what they had in mind. Rabbit was the first one to speak.

'I think we should continue on our search. We've come so far; it would be a shame to give up now. Mouse needs our help and I must admit I'm quite enjoying myself. I've never been on an adventure before.'

'I'm enjoying the fresh air,' Mole added nervously.

Vole gazed dreamily towards the old ruined castle.

'To think I might be lying in my furry pocket, all by myself, sleeping.'

Rabbit poked him.

'But *of course* I would much rather be going on an adventure,' Vole added quickly.

Five forky - tailies turned up their forked tails bravely.

'That's it, then,' said Rabbit. He swallowed hard. He secretly wished he hadn't met Mouse that morning but he decided to keep that very much to himself.

'We're all agreed. Lead on forky - tailies!'

The brave little friends, for friends they now were, marched out of the garden, down a rocky slope and followed the forky - tailies to a small, dark cave in the hillside. As they crept into the entrance it smelled damp and felt icy cold. Vole shivered and Rabbit hugged himself to keep warm.

The darkness was unwelcoming and Rabbit and Vole, who couldn't see anything at all, grasped the hard, rough surface of the cave walls to feel their way along. Mouse followed Mole, who was more confident and used to dark places. As Mole and Mouse scampered along behind the forky - tailies, Rabbit held on firmly to Mouse's tail. Vole was last and fretted that he might just be left behind. The five forky - tailies twitched their antennae and chattered excitedly.

'Nearly there,' said the fifth forky - tailie, who was now leading as the first forky - tailie.

'Won't be long,' said Para the second forky - tailie who used to be the fourth.

'I can see light ahead,' said the third forky - tailie who was always third and quite happy to be right in the middle of any exploring that had to be done. The last two forky - tailies who had lost their positions at the front were quite happy to be at the end of the line. They were in no hurry to meet whatever was lying ahead.

Suddenly, everyone stopped and looked towards something sparkling and shining in the darkness. The first forky - tailie pointed to a silver coin lying on the floor. It was glinting in the light of a flickering candle.

'Look! Is that your squeak?' asked all forky - tailies at once.

The animals looked. They couldn't see very clearly but they knew it wasn't Mouse's squeak. They shook their heads sadly. The coin was, indeed, as shiny and bright as a sparkling jewel but it wasn't loud or furry or sweet smelling or purple. Mole, who was, as we know, quite used to dark, damp places, shook with fear; he could sense danger. As his friends got used to the lack of light in the cave they too knew that they were not alone. It didn't take them long to realise that this was a very, very dangerous place indeed.

They were now in the deepest part of the cave and everywhere they looked cats were lying around on ledges, sleeping or stretching, climbing or cleaning themselves with their long tongues. Black cats, ginger cats, thin cats, fat cats, longhaired cats and shorthaired cats, all kinds of cats. An old, bent figure sat on a wooden, rickety chair counting his silver coins. The coins were heaped in piles and balanced in towers, spread over the surface of a small table as a greedy miser counted them one by one. Each coin sparkled as the light from an old lamp shone on the secret treasure. One very large, black cat sat beside the old man, licking her paws. Her long, furry tail twitched as she looked slowly round to the edge of the cave. The sharp-eyed creature saw the friends watching from the shadows and licked her lips.

'He gets into a terrible temper,' she hissed, showing her sharp, yellow teeth.

'That means you will have to be *quiet* too!' joined in the large black cat glaring at them with staring, green eyes.

'Shall I quieten them now or shall we hide them away?' asked the ginger cat holding out a very large, threatening paw.

'Miaow!' they all cried together.

Rabbit shook from head to tail.

Vole covered his eyes with his paws and Mole hid behind Rabbit.

The old man shuffled over to the gathering group of cats.

'Off wi' ye,' he shouted as all the cats ran back to the ledges which frilled the cave.

'Wha meddles wi' me?' asked the old man peering into the darkness.

The five forky tailies scuttled into the shadows as Mouse stepped forward into the light of the flickering candle.

'Ah, a wee mousie. No wonder ma cats were fussing so; I cannae blame them for being well pleased to meet ye,' he laughed.

Rabbit crept out of the darkness.

'Ah! Won't ye make a lovely rabbit stew,' suggested the old man bending down low to take a closer look. Rabbit hopped sideways to avoid his grasp and there stood Mole shivering from head to toe.

'A mole! Lovely smooth moleskin could make warm linings for ma gloves.'

Vole still had his paws over his eyes. He couldn't see the old man but he heard everything.

'And ye ma wee laddie,' he said, pointing a gnarled finger at Vole, 'could line the fingers!'

Five forky - tailies scurried about trying to find a way out.

'And as for ye five forky - tailies; one swat and you'd be gone!' He chuckled to see the little group of friends shaking with fear.

Mouse was so sorry that she had led her friends into such trouble. She had got them into such a mess; it was up to her to get them out of it.

'We're very sorry for coming into your cave,' she said bravely, 'but we were looking for ma squeak.'

'And why should I be bothered about ye and yer squeak?' asked the old man.

'Well sir, ma squeak is very, very loud!'

'Does na bother me.'

'Ma squeak is soft and furry.'

The old man shrugged his shoulders. 'So?'

'Ma squeak smells of sweet tea and rosewater.'

The old man wrinkled his nose.

'Ma squeak is a lovely warm colour like ripe plums.'

'Ma cats want to know if yer squeak is tasty,' croaked the old man, 'cos' ma cats get hungry!'

'Oh yes sir, ma squeak is very, very tasty,' answered mouse nervously.

'And I bet every other little bit of you is tasty too,' added the large, black cat who had crept nearer to listen.

'I wonder what I should do with ye, creeping into ma cave like that and disturbing me. I dinnae like being disturbed!'

Mouse was feeling even braver now.

'Well sir,' answered Mouse, 'Whatever you decide is fine but please, please, please don't send us back to the castle.'

'And what dinnae ye like about the castle?'

'Well sir a terrible, scaly, red eyed dragon lives there now and we all had to leave. He was so scary and bad tempered; all he's interested in is his gold.'

'And does he have much gold?' asked the old miser as he glanced towards his own pile of money stacked up on the table.

'Oh yes and he's on the look out for more,' added Mouse opening her eyes wide.

The old man's face twitched. 'He cannae have as much as me.'

'Oh lots more money sir, but he is still not satisfied.'

The old miser was showing more interest at the mention of money.

'Oh no,' shivered Mouse, putting her hands over her ears.

Mole and Vole were holding each other tightly.

Rabbit put his paws over his ears too.

'Can you not hear?' asked Mouse.

'Hear what?' said the old man. 'That's only the wind howling around the door of ma cave.'

'Oh no sir! I know that sound anywhere. That's the sound of the dragon's wings flapping and whooshing through the air. He has followed us!'

The cats began to cry loudly and became very restless. Some leapt from ledge to ledge. Others ran across the cave spilling their saucers of milk and knocking over chairs and boxes, which were lying around. The old man, being the miser that he was, ran to save his money. As he frantically pushed his coins into a large chest he could be heard muttering,

'Ye dinnae ken; no one's getting ma money, not even a dragon!'

Neither he, nor the cats heard Rabbit shout 'Run!'

Neither did they see the Rabbit, Mole, Vole, and Mouse follow five forky - tailies out of the cave and into the daylight. The friends ran and ran as fast as they could back to the ruins of the old castle, back home, safe and sound.

'You were so brave Mouse,' said Rabbit.

'And so clever!' said Mole.

'I don't know how you could speak to that old miser,' said Vole with such admiration.

'What a story!' said the first forky -tailie.

'Fancy thinking about a dragon,' said the second forky - tailie.

'A dragon who liked gold was such a clever idea!' added the third forky - tailie.

'I'm only sorry we didn't find your squeak,' sighed the fourth forky - tailie.

'Eek!' shouted Mouse with a sudden leap into the air.

The fifth forky - tailie jumped with her.

'She's found her squeak! Listen to her!'

Mouse was squeaking loudly and clearly, over and over again.

The little mouse ran into the bushes and a few minutes later she was seen pulling out a very sleepy, brown, bedraggled mouse by his paw. He was wearing a purple kilt and waistcoat and was the smartest mouse the friends had ever seen.

'Here he is; here's ma Squeak.'

Squeak was bigger than Mouse. He gave a loud chuckle causing the buttons to pop on his purple waistcoat. As he walked out of the long grass a waft of sweet tea and rosewater drifted across to the friends standing together on the path. They smiled at Squeak as Mouse scolded him for disappearing like that.

'What were you doing in the long grass? I was worried about you.'

'I was hiding,' said Squeak.

'Why?' asked Mouse.

'I was hiding from the dragon.'

'What dragon?' asked Mouse. All the friends looked at Squeak in horror.

'The dragon who has just moved into the castle. You know; the one who is so keen on his gold.'

He grinned a huge grin and gave such a loud chuckle. A very, very loud chuckle, the loudest anyone had ever heard.

Mouse was right; her Squeak was loud!

All the friends joined in and the sound of their laughter echoed all around the castle walls. The miser and cats, living in the cave nearby, shuddered as they heard the sound and thinking that the dragon was coming, they packed up their belongings and left, never to be seen again.

Mouse cried and cried but this time not with sadness but with tears of joy.

She had found courage that she never knew existed, she had found eight wonderful new friends and, most important of all, she had found her Squeak.

Hilda-

a cautionary tale

Hilda dumped her bag in the hall

Threw down her coat, sang her usual call

'I'm home! I'm starving! What's for tea?'
And Mum answered 'Patience
Just wait and see!'
Hilda plonked herself in front of the telly
And ate a huge bag full of strawberry jellies
When dinner - time came Hilda's tummy was bulging
Packed to the brim, through too much indulging
It was corned beef hash for dinner
And Hilda pulled a face
She dragged the chair and kicked it
As she sat down in her place
She was too full for her dinner
Corned - beef hash made her feel ill
'I'm not eating that awful stuff!' she said
But Mum said, 'Yes you will!'
Hilda pushed her dinner round
Lined up her sprouts to have a race
'That does it,' shouted Granddad

'Hilda! You're a terrible disgrace!'

She stuck her tongue out at her brother

Frowned and muttered at her mother

Turned her nose up at the hash

Squashed her sprouts into a mash

Piled the meat - mix in degrees

Into mountains, topped with peas

Knocked her glass and spilled her juice

Asked for afters, chocolate mousse!

Chocolate mousse, her favourite pud

But Mum just shook her head

Your behaviour has been far from good

And so I'm sending you to bed!

Hilda grimaced, shook and trembled
Glared at Granddad, turned quite red
Pulled her very worst of faces
'You'll stay like that!' he said.

'Oh dear, our Hilda's come over all funny

'Run to the bathroom dear,' suggested her granny

Hilda felt sick and her poo was all runny

She had a terrible pain in her tummy

She sat on the loo sulking and glaring

All goggle-eyed and angrily staring

She twisted her mouth and wrinkled her nose

Bared all her teeth and curled up her toes

She thought about Granddad and what he had said

As both her cheeks burned a fiery red

Then suddenly without warning

She was covered in scaly skin

Her body started twisting

And became quite long and thin

Her back it arched and sprouted wings

As she decreased in size

She became the worst of horrid things

With great, big, bloodshot eyes

Because she was so light and small

She skidded down the banister

And landed in the hall

She sat before the cat flap

As Puss came in for tea

Puss hissed, Hilda cried

'Don't pounce it's only me!'

Hilda's family were having dinner

They were totally unaware

That Hilda was metamorphosing

A condition very rare

She felt they wouldn't care

Even if they knew

So that is why she crawled away

To where the blackberries grew

She sat beneath the berries

And cried and cried and cried

She met a worm and gave a squirm

Then eagerly replied

'I have no wish to stay here

I belong inside!

This is not me! I went all wrong!'

She very sadly sighed

The worm just couldn't see her

And continued on his way

He wriggled down into the soil

Hilda hoped that he would stay

She was feeling very lonely

As a wasp flew overhead

'What an ugly, little beast'

It impolitely said

Hilda nodded haughtily

And pointed to her house

'That's where it all started'

She muttered to a mouse

The mouse sat down to listen

'It was in the dining room

The place where all my troubles

Started just this afternoon'

An earwig dropped down beside her

With a heavy thud

A soldier beetle and a bee

Both settled in the mud

A woodlouse and a grasshopper came

A ladybird and fly

A butterfly with gaudy wings

That had just been passing by

They came to share good company

Hear a story, take a nap

They didn't see the spider

Preparing to set her trap

Working with guile and expert skill

Weaving without a sound

She spun her silk with gentle care

And quietly tiptoed round

The spider planned her meal so fine

Considered the ones on which she'd dine

She liked the juicy, grubby fly

The woodlouse and the butterfly

'The grasshopper and beetles plump

May be a tender bit of rump

If I could avoid a nasty sting

A bee might be a tasty thing

I'll keep my distance from the mouse

And that weird creature from the house'

It did not appeal in any way

She wished that it would go away

She pounced and wrapped each tasty feast

'I'll soon be rid of that ugly beast

I'll tie it up, leave it a while

I'm sure its juices taste quite vile'

She glared at Hilda pulled a face

As if to put her in her place

But Hilda guessed the spider's plan

'I'll have to work as best I can

I have to save us from this fate

Or we'll be a meal on a spider's plate'

She admired the spider

And the clever web she made

Her trickery and cunning

And the table she had laid

But this was not a time to pause

To admire a spider's skills

This was a time of danger

A battle between two wills

She said, 'Don't pull that face at me

We're not going to be a spider's tea!'

Hilda stood tall with face bright red

'You'll stay like that,' she bravely said

Then suddenly without warning

Off came the scaly skin

Her body started twisting

And became itself again

Her back stretched out and lost its wings

As she increased in size

Her face became the prettiest thing

With happy, laughing eyes

The silken thread which held them fast

Tore and fell apart

The little creatures got away

And Hilda with a heavy heart

Walked up the path

To eat her tea

And say that she was sorry

To all her family

For her tantrum and her nasty face

She knew she'd still be in disgrace

She walked back home

Stood tall and proud

Addressed the family

Right out aloud

She told her tale about her friends

Who nearly came to a sticky end

She looked straight at her Granddad

And to his great surprise

She pulled the very best of faces

'You'll stay like that,' he cried

And for once Hilda believed him

And said sorry for all she'd done

She promised to hold her temper

And try to help her mum

She wouldn't eat too many sweets

Especially before her tea

And like the spider she would wait

Very, very patiently.

Halloween Mouse

Chapter 1

Kate pulled the duvet up over her face and hid in the darkness. She listened to the family laughing downstairs and the clatter of dishes as everyone tidied up after the party. She was feeling very tired after a wonderful time lighting pumpkins and playing 'trick or treat' with friends and family. Mum had made cakes decorated as white ghosts and orange pumpkins and Auntie Joan had brought a green jelly topped with pears. The pears had liquorice tails and whiskers and chocolate ears and looked just like real mice. Her little cousin Jack had worn an ugly purple mask and brandished a plastic three-pronged fork all evening. He had tried to frighten her so she had played along and pretended to be terrified; he chased her round the house and they laughed hysterically while posing for Dad's camera.

Kate's pumpkin now sat in the corner of the room looking at her with a silly grin on its face. It had looked good with a candle lit inside; translucent and quite spooky with its crooked tooth lying at an angle in the centre of its mouth. Kate lay in bed imagining spiders dropping from their webs, swinging on silken threads and witches flying on broomsticks. She was convinced that tonight she could quite easily have nightmares.

Suddenly she heard a terrifying scream and a loud bang as something fell, with a crash, to the floor. Was it a witch? Was it a ghost? She listened from under her duvet. She heard the crash of a saucepan and then Auntie Joan letting out a short, loud scream. Dad's voice, firm and clear, announced that a trap would be set. Voices called 'goodnight' and then there was absolute silence. It didn't take Kate long to realise that everyone downstairs had, to quell Auntie's fears, agreed to set a trap to catch a mouse. No one in the whole world had spared a thought for the poor mouse, no one that is, except Kate. She tossed and turned but sleep was out of the question. A small brown, furry mouse with ears erect and whiskers twitching was very soon going to walk across Mum's clean, polished floor, sniff the bacon and walk straight into Dad's trap.

Kate had to do something quickly. She pushed the bed covers back, wrapped her dressing gown around her and tiptoed downstairs. The light from the sitting room shone along the bottom of the door. Luckily Mum and Dad were watching the TV and didn't hear Kate creep past. She opened the dining room door quietly and peeped into the kitchen. There, in the centre of the floor was a tangled slice of greasy, bacon wrapped round the trap ready to catch the unsuspecting creature. Kate looked around, behind, and in between, every place she could think of but she found no sign of a mouse. What was she to do? Her family wouldn't help; it was they who set the trap. It was dark outside; no one would be near to give a hand. Her brother was in bed and her cousins had gone home.

Within minutes she had an idea. She ran upstairs and drew back her bedroom curtains excitedly. The stars were twinkling in the cold night sky and the trees waved their branches in a welcoming response to her searching gaze. A cat cried in the silence as tin cans and bottles fell out of next door's dustbins. As Kate peered through the window, a collection of grey shapes caught her eye as they swirled and meandered between distant buildings. As these dark shadows crept closer, they appeared to be moving more quickly and urgently as they passed by. Kate could hear laughter and calling to one another as if they were in a hurry. Kate called out to them but her cries were ignored and the shadows moved on.

Chapter 2

Kate waved, pleadingly; she was hoping that one of them would take notice. Soon a dark shadow turned from the others and rushed towards Kate's bedroom window.

'Can I help?' asked the lady dressed in purple and black and sitting proudly on a broomstick.

Kate thought she had a beautiful face, kind eyes and a nicely curved mouth. Her nose was sharp and pointed and her chin was very long but she had an inner glow, which made her look particularly striking.

'I have to save a mouse,' pleaded Kate, 'from Dad's trap. Auntie Joan doesn't like mice and there's some bacon and, oh dear,' spluttered Kate.

'I see,' answered the witch calmly. 'I'm off to a party at the moment. It's Halloween you know.' Kate nodded.

'Well, I'm not sure whether I have time for this but I shall do what I can.'

Her broomstick stopped in mid air and the witch (Kate noted her pointed hat and black cloak) stepped gracefully on to the windowsill and, with toes pointed, she glided on to the bed. Sitting cross-legged she clicked her long, bony fingers and the bedroom door flew open. A breeze blew across the landing and, as autumn leaves are carried by the wind, so too, was a little mouse with eyes wide and tail quivering, swept unwittingly into the palm of the witch's hand. The witch smiled kindly at the mouse and introduced herself.

'Hello, I'm Griselda, Zelda for short. This young lady is Kate,' she added, presenting the mouse to Kate as if it were a prize trophy.

'Can you look after him now?' asked the witch.

Kate stared at the fact that she knew her name. She also stared at the thought of caring for a mouse. She wasn't too sure. She'd always wanted a pet but she'd always considered a cat or a dog or even a rabbit. But a mouse? What would her parents say? Kate nodded without even thinking about the situation properly. The witch climbed onto her broomstick and pulling her hat down closer to her head, lifting her collar against the biting wind she wished them both a very good night and waved goodbye. As she flew out of sight Kate secretly wished that she hadn't gone. She'd never met a real witch before and Zelda seemed just the kind of witch Mum and Dad would, perhaps, consider acceptable. It struck Kate that Zelda was not at all like the witches she had met in her storybooks and so she came to the conclusion that she must have been a good witch and not the least bit wicked. Kate looked down at the mouse sitting in the palm of her hand. What was she going to do with it? Where was it going to sleep? What on earth was Mum going to say? Kate had no answers. She set the mouse down on the carpet while she thought things through. The mouse was obviously making itself at home as it gnawed at the edges of the bedside rug. Was it nesting?

'Oh dear, I hope you're not about to have babies,' warned Kate, climbing into bed.

The sheets were cold so Kate curled up tightly to get warm. She could hear the scurrying of the mouse as it scampered around the room and she secretly wished, just for a fleeting moment, that she hadn't bothered trying to save the mouse after all.

It was then that she heard a tapping on the bedroom window. Peeping through the curtains she could see that the wind was still blowing and that it had started raining. A dark figure was clinging to the window frame. Zelda! Her hair was wet and bedraggled, her pointed hat now floppy and misshapen, as she grinned at Kate, displaying an absence of three teeth from each side of her smile. She looked very comical but at the same time, very approachable and Kate rushed to help her into the comfort of her room.

'I missed the party because of that mouse!' said Zelda as she glared at the poor little creature huddled in the corner of the room. Kate shuddered.

'Oh dear,' she thought. 'Have I saved this poor mouse just for it to be subject to an even worse fate?'

Chapter 3

Kate looked at the mouse in alarm and the small creature returned a similar expression. Neither of them needed to worry. Zelda pulled off her hat, and shook her long, jet-black flowing hair behind her.

'Thank goodness,' she sighed. 'I didn't want to go to the party anyway and you were the best excuse I had. It's tradition to have a party every Halloween and we're all expected to attend. I have never enjoyed them; I get so tired of sitting around cauldrons and chanting silly spells. They spend most of the time talking about the olden days, coughing and spluttering over their potions and playing silly games.'

'Won't you get into trouble?' asked Kate. She was concerned that Zelda was now being a bit of a rebel.

'I've always been a bit of a rebel witch,' added Zelda as if she had been reading Kate's mind.

'My name apparently means patience and obedience, of which neither applies to me. Mother says I've been like it since I was a child. I didn't like putting spiders and bats wings into the soup because I always preferred plain vegetable.'

'And croutons.' added Kate suddenly feeling very hungry. Zelda nodded.

'I wasn't very good at remembering spells either,' continued Zelda. 'No patience to learn properly you see. I still can't. I'm always making mistakes.'

'Did you have to go to school?' asked Kate, with interest.

'Oh yes. Being a witch is not easy. It takes years of learning and lots of practice. I'm a big disappointment to my family because I've always been bottom of the class. I'd rather go dancing or watch TV, and I have lots of hobbies such as pressing flowers and stamp collecting. Anyway, I'm here now. I can catch up with them later. I was late for a good reason, wasn't I?' Zelda looked down at the mouse.

'Mind you, I'm not sure whether they'd approve of me saving a mouse. My dear family would probably be more delighted if I gave it to Bainbridge.'

'Bainbridge?' queried Kate.

'My cat,' answered Zelda.

The poor little mouse, still huddled in the corner, shuddered at the thought.

'Now, we need to find you a home,' said Zelda gently, picking up the mouse and tickling it under its chin.

'Oh dear,' thought Kate, 'she's not going to try a spell is she?'

And sure enough she did!

'Caldi housey, homeless mousie find a hole, burrow like mole wrangle quangle tousie,' she chanted in a strange, eerie voice. Within seconds a crack appeared in the skirting board.

'Oh, that was supposed to be a hole,' complained Zelda, with a surprised expression.

'The mouse will never get through that. I'll try again.'

Zelda repeated almost identical words with the result that a hole appeared, as desired, but not a round, semi-circular hole especially for a mouse but a hole in the shape of a house, roof, chimney and all. Zelda laughed.

' A house hole. This could start quite a fashion. Mouse. Meet your new home.'

The mouse gave a squeak and ran into its new house hole, very much relieved. Kate looked at Zelda. She couldn't help thinking that, for a witch, she was so very pretty. Her hair was extremely long and very beautiful; she almost reminded her of Rapunzel, and her eyes, so large and dark were edged with the blackest of silk eyelashes. She had soft, curved lips and delicate pink cheeks.

'It's a shame about your teeth and nose,' Kate remarked, without thinking. 'You should get your teeth seen to; it's marvellous what they can do these days and…my Auntie's a nurse in plastic surgery…you could get a nose job.'

Chapter 4

Kate looked sheepishly at her visitor.

'You really are lovely, you know.'

Kate blushed. Had she said too much? Zelda beamed.

'I've always wanted to have a nose job but Mother says it doesn't go with the job. A witch is supposed to have these imperfections otherwise she doesn't look like a witch. The trouble is, you see, I don't want to be a witch. I've got ambitions. I want to be a model.'

Kate stared. Zelda's mood was now changing. Kate could see that the whole conversation had touched a nerve so she announced quickly that she would go to get some supper. She tiptoed once again, downstairs. She could hear the TV still on in the sitting room and mutterings between the grown ups alongside the clinking of glasses. Kate could understand, in a funny way, just how Zelda felt. There were often times when Kate wanted to do something different but grown ups always disapproved.

'I bet Zelda's Halloween parties were just like afternoon tea at Grandma's.'

Kate loved Grandma dearly but she often found it a strain trying to be quiet and polite and not move around in case she knocked the china.

'Go and run outside dear, run off some energy until teatime,' was always the answer and Kate, who didn't feel like running around, was sent outside in the cold.

'Yes,' she thought to herself, she knew just how Zelda was feeling.

'It's probably just as well I called her to help otherwise she'd have had to go to that beastly party,' she reassured herself. Kate decided to give her a delicious supper to celebrate, a supper fit for a queen – no – a witch.

Kate and Zelda sat, cross-legged on the floor and shared a wonderful supper. Sausage rolls, jam and cream sandwich cake, blackberry pie and left over pear mice and jelly, all washed down with ice-cold milk. The mouse, too, ventured out of his house hole and sat nearby eating the crumbs, which they piled up before him. Kate told Zelda about her family, her little cousin Jack who tormented her incessantly and her big brother Ben who was growing up fast and didn't always like 'little sister' round. She adored them all and looked forward to introducing them to her new friend. She told her about school and her friends and her favourite TV programmes. Zelda told Kate about all the spells she couldn't get right and about her schoolteacher who was a very strict witch in the traditional way, warts, and green face and all, who despaired of her. They chatted well past Kate's parents' bedtime. The television was switched off; Mum and Dad locked up and went upstairs closing their bedroom door quietly. All was dark except for the light from Kate's bedside lamp and still the two friends continued talking. The clock downstairs struck midnight and Kate soon realised that Halloween was over.

'It's the 1st of November,' she smiled. A look of panic came across Zelda's face.

'They'll be coming back from the party. Quick! Where's my broomstick? I must join them.'

They switched the bedroom light out and opened the curtains. It wasn't long before dark, misshapen shadows floated over the rooftops, dipping and swaying as they flew home. Kate felt a lump in her throat. She hadn't known Zelda long but she liked her very much. She knew, at that moment, more than anything else, that she didn't want her to go.

Chapter 5

Zelda gazed towards the witches' shadows returning home for another year. The rebel rose inside her.

'No, I'm staying!' she announced firmly. 'I'll stay here for a while and catch up with them later. I could do with some time off this witching caper.'

Kate gulped. She was absolutely thrilled that Zelda was staying but how was she going to explain her to Mum and Dad. Would they approve of having a real witch to stay?

Kate showed Zelda to the spare room. She lent her new friend one of Mum's warm, fluffy, nightdresses, and whispered goodnight, closing the bedroom door behind her.

'I've never had a Halloween like it,' thought Kate. 'I must be dreaming.'

She pinched herself just to make sure. No, it was real.

'I wonder what the morning will bring?' she said to herself as she snuggled under the duvet for the third time that evening. As she was dropping off to sleep, she heard the mouse scuttle into its house hole, safe and content.

'It's all your fault,' sighed Kate as she drifted away to yet more adventures in her dreams.

The next morning Kate was late down to breakfast.

'Good morning, young lady or should I say good afternoon,' called Dad from the sitting room. 'Your friend has been up for hours.'

'I've just made Zelda a nice cup of coffee,' announced Mum, carrying a tray into the dining room. 'What would you like dear?'

Kate followed her mother to find Zelda sitting in Granddad's favourite chair at the table. She was reading a magazine quite contentedly. Kate looked puzzled.

'It's alright,' said Zelda in answer to her friend's expression.

'I've explained I'm here for a while, and that I'm a witch on vacation, so to speak. They took it really well, along with a little helping of magic! I'm getting better, my spells do sometimes work.'

Kate was relieved that she didn't have too much explaining to do and helped herself to a bowl of cornflakes. Perhaps things might get back to normal sooner than she had anticipated.

'Did you catch that mouse Andrew?' Mum called suddenly to Dad.

'No, it must have decided not to come in again,' answered Dad. 'Good job too!'

Kate looked to her cornflakes. How was she going to explain the house hole? Once again Zelda read her thoughts.

'Don't worry. They won't see it; it's invisible. Just a little bit of magic –again. I can see I'm going to have fun practising my spells here.'

Kate cringed.

'Oh dear, do you think you should?' she asked. 'I thought you were giving yourself a holiday away from bewitching. Besides, they don't always go right, do they?' Zelda shrugged her shoulders.

'Maybe I'll just keep it for the sticky moments, ok?' Zelda stood up as she said this, looked in the mirror and smiled. The gaps in her teeth looked worse in the light of day and Kate's remarks from the night before came back to her.

'Kate, do you think you could get your magician to fix my teeth, fill in the gaps?' Zelda asked turning to Kate hopefully.

'Why can't you fix them yourself?' asked Kate. 'After all you are a witch!'

Zelda explained that she'd never been allowed to learn the spell for changing one's appearance.

'Not thought suitable,' grinned Zelda.

'Well, my teeth fixer is not a magician! He's a dentist,' answered Kate 'and yes, he'll do it for you but you'll have to pay for such treatment.'

'Now that's where I'll have to resort to a little spell,' added Zelda. 'That could be a very sticky moment don't you agree?' Kate almost agreed and promised to make an appointment for her as soon as possible.

Chapter 6

Kate was pleased that she still had a few days of the half term school holiday left to spend with her new friend. The days that followed were great fun. Zelda was taken on visits to the library, the museum, the Cathedral and the local shopping centre. They tried on clothes, hats, and jewellery and sampled expensive perfumes in the big stores. They had lunch out at burger bars and big store restaurants and fed ducks by the river. Everywhere they went people stared. Zelda enjoyed the attention and remarked that this was something she would have to get used to if she was to become a model. Kate was less pleased. She was annoyed at the way people muttered under their breath about Zelda's nose and the way they giggled at her deep purple dress flowing around her ankles, her black cloak and her high-heeled boots. When Zelda smiled people stood, open mouthed at the sight, which Kate considered extremely rude.

'Why couldn't they see Zelda for the pleasant, friendly person she was, her mild manner and her kind gestures rather than what she looked like,' thought Kate. 'She's a lovely person, she's my friend, and looks aren't everything!'

It was at that moment that Kate became overcome with a terrible feeling of guilt. Wasn't it she who had prompted the idea of a dental appointment and a nose job so that her friend could look just right? She was horrified at herself. She turned to Zelda, who was busying herself amongst the postcards looking for an exciting picture to send to her family.

'Zelda, you don't have to get your teeth done, nor do you need a nose job. I like you just the way you are,' pointed out Kate with enthusiasm. Zelda answered with just as much enthusiasm.

'Oh no, I'm looking forward to a new me. It will be such a shock for them when I get home. And I do so like to shock people,' giggled Zelda.

On Thursday morning Kate took Zelda to the dentist, as promised, and waited for her downstairs in the waiting room. The minutes ticked by and Kate picked up various magazines to read but they did not hold her interest for long. She looked over, towards the receptionist, as if to question the time the dentist was taking to see to Zelda.

'Don't worry, she won't be long,' reassured the receptionist as she peeped her head around the hatch door of her office. She smiled a wide, beaming smile towards Kate. Kate gasped in horror as a very deep desire to run surged inside her. The receptionist's huge, friendly smile had three teeth missing from each side and the positions of these open spaces looked strangely familiar.

'Oh no, what has Zelda been up to?' muttered Kate to herself.

A few minutes later Zelda arrived downstairs, wearing the 'perfect' smile. No gaps were visible and her teeth sparkled. Kate grabbed Zelda's arm.

'I think it's time we were going,' advised Kate, pulling her new friend out of the dentists. She ran home as fast as she could, forcibly dragging Zelda behind her.

When they arrived home Kate frowned at her friend, pointing out that she had some explaining to do. Zelda could tell that Kate was not very pleased with her.

'Well?' asked Kate, as she flopped onto the settee with exhaustion. Zelda looked sheepishly at Kate.

'Well. Your dentist was very nice,' she explained 'but after examining my teeth and making plaster moulds of my mouth he said it would take a few weeks before he could make my new teeth and fit them properly. I couldn't wait weeks. I tried to explain that I was only here for a short time and that I had to fly home in a few days but I couldn't convince him. He told me to go down and make a new appointment with the receptionist for three weeks time and recommended that I postpone my flight. It was then that I remembered a spell my old granny once taught me. It was one of the few spells I could do well. So easy!'

'Yes?' responded Kate in a questioning voice.

'Well, it's much easier to move something from one place to another than to make something completely new and I had noticed, when I came in, that the lady behind the glass doors had a lovely smile.'

'Oh no, the poor woman, how could you?'

Chapter 7

Kate was not pleased. Zelda knew that she had upset her new friend; she wanted to make amends.

'If it's any consolation she's in good hands; he's a good dentist.'

'That's it, I'm not taking you to get your nose done. Goodness knows what chaos you could cause in a hospital. Anyway, as you have so eagerly pointed out, that will be a lengthy period of treatment too and you just don't have the time!' Kate jumped up to pour herself a glass of lemonade. She poured one for Zelda too, but rather reluctantly.

'I'm sorry,' apologised Zelda. 'Tell you what. I'll write to my Granny; she's a whiz with her spells. She'll put things right for your lady at the dentist, I'm sure she will.'

'I certainly hope so,' added Kate sharply. 'Now, how about helping me to lay the table for tea. Mum will be in soon.'

The two friends quietly laid the table but neither said very much at all. When Mum and Dad came in from shopping at the supermarket, they ate their tea in silence.

'Ben will be late home this evening,' announced Mum. 'He's gone to meet James from the station. He has a few weeks study leave.'

Kate's eyes lit up. She adored her cousin James. He was a lot older than her and was away at college. In the excitement she quite forgot how cross she had been feeling with Zelda.

'You'll like James,' said Kate turning to her friend, 'he's training to be a vet. He's always loved animals. He'll love our mouse,' she told Zelda.

Zelda wasn't listening. She was gazing thoughtfully at an ornament standing on a glass cabinet in the corner of the room. The tall, china figure of a goose girl stood between the family photographs in the centre. It had always been a particular favourite of Mum's; she had always remarked on how pretty the girl looked. Kate nudged her friend. She could see that the imminent arrival of cousin James had not made much impression. Zelda turned her face towards Kate and smiled. Kate looked at Zelda and then at her mother's favourite china figure. She gave a sigh.

'Oh no!' she remarked to herself. 'I hope Mum doesn't notice.'

The goose girl had miraculously developed a rather prominent, hooked nose.

'You look well today dear,' chirped in Mum, looking at Zelda, 'have you had your hair done?'

Zelda smiled politely. 'I've just been making a few changes, Mrs T.'

'Well, they suit you dear.'

Kate had to agree. Zelda was now very pretty and obviously very pleased with herself. At that moment they heard laughing in the hall as the front door slammed shut.

'James!' Kate shouted as she jumped up in excitement and ran to meet her favourite cousin. She threw her arms around his neck.

'Hello you. Fancy putting up with me for a few days?'

Kate grinned. She could 'put up' with James any time. She led him by the hand into the sitting room.

'Come on you'll have to meet a new friend of mine, she's a real w…w… witch.'

'Hey, that's no way to talk about a friend. I wonder what you call me when I'm away?' he laughed.

As she entered the room, Kate stopped in her tracks. She suddenly realised that Zelda, apart from her strange clothes, no longer looked like a witch and to introduce her as such a thing was now a very poor description.

'James,' smiled Kate, 'meet Zelda.'

She grimaced and looked at James for a reaction. She could plainly see that any words she might have uttered would not have been heard at all.

'Oh no,' complained Kate. 'He's gone all soppy on me.'

Sure enough, the sight of Zelda had caused James to be quite speechless for the first time in his life. Zelda too, had been overcome when she set eyes on James. She felt that she was a witch no longer. Now she was a princess and this was definitely her Prince Charming. The only thing Kate could think right at that moment was that things were just going from bad to worse, getting complicated and that she had never experienced anything quite like it before. Once again, she pinched herself to check that this was all very real. She was right in the middle of a witch/fairy story and now that James had entered into the plot, she had a sneaky feeling that the happy ending she had hoped for was not going to be quite the ending she had expected. The words floated round in her head. 'Princess Zelda and Prince James lived happily ever after.' Oh no! She was very fond of Zelda but she couldn't possibly allow James to fall in love and marry her witch!

Everyone now had fallen into an interesting conversation of which Kate was not obviously a part so the only thing for her to do was to say goodnight and go to bed. As she closed the door, Zelda, with James hanging on her every word, was discussing the merits of old time dancing, waltz, foxtrot and quickstep, and was plainly in control. James remarked that he should have watched 'Strictly Come Dancing' on the telly then he would have been better informed.

As Kate climbed into bed she saw a long, pink tail just disappearing into the house hole. Yes, it all started with a mouse.

'It's all your fault,' she said accusingly. 'All your fault – again!'

Chapter 8

Monday 3.30pm and Kate ran excitedly out of school. Zelda had promised she would come to meet her and so, as soon as the school bell rang, Kate ran along the corridor, grabbed her coat and bag from the cloakroom and charged outside. She had not told anyone that a witch was picking her up from school. She knew that they wouldn't have believed her and besides, she felt, just for a while, that she didn't really want to share her new friend with anyone. Even James' attention was not, as Kate put it, very welcome. Sure enough, there was Zelda, standing at the school gate. She waved to Kate and grinned. As Kate ran towards her she realised why her witch friend had looked so excited.

'I thought I'd give you a lift home. It makes a nice change from walking every day.' Kate gulped. 'A broomstick!' Zelda had brought her broomstick and they were going to ride home on it. Just at that moment Claudia Patterson, a girl from Kate's class passed by.

'What a shame you didn't get picked,' Claudia said to Kate, looking down her nose in a superior way. 'You looked so nice in that purple skirt. Better luck next time eh?' Kate scowled and Zelda could see that Kate was not very pleased.

'What was that about?' asked Zelda.

'The PTA is putting on a fashion show,' explained Kate 'and Claudia was chosen to be one of the models. I wasn't. Claudia is just showing off and I don't care anyway,' added Kate indignantly. Zelda could see that Kate didn't mean a word of it and needed cheering up.

'Come on. Climb aboard. I bet Madame Claudia hasn't travelled home on a broomstick before.'

Everyone standing nearby, parents, children, teachers, all looked on in astonishment as Zelda chanted some magic words. The broomstick floated upwards, turned and shot forwards in the direction of home. Claudia stood, open-mouthed as she looked up and saw Kate passing overhead on a broomstick. Kate remarked that seeing Claudia so aghast at such a sight was worth fifty chances of being a model at the PTA fashion show. Zelda was very quiet as they alighted on the front lawn and went into the house for tea. Kate was so excited over the ride on Zelda's broomstick that she had quite forgotten the school fashion show. Zelda, however, had not, and so, as soon as tea was over, she started quizzing Kate about the whole affair. She asked questions about the venue, who was in charge, what was it in aid of, could she get a ticket? Kate explained that the school needed new computers so the PTA had offered to stage a fashion show, with refreshments, to raise the funds. Kate could see a sparkle in Zelda's eyes.

'Oh no!' sighed Kate.

Chapter 9

It had not taken Kate long to realise why Zelda was showing so much interest in the school fashion show. Of course. Her witch had always wanted to be a model. Kate shook her head.

'They've chosen all the models they need. They really don't need anymore. I tell you what, I'll buy three tickets as Mum would like to come too, and we'll go to watch.'

Zelda nodded in agreement but Kate could see that her friend's thoughts were scheming yet another plot to change the natural way of things. Kate resolved not to ask any questions even though she was a little concerned. She knew that, in time, all would be revealed. Kate crossed her fingers tightly. 'Just in case, because, well, just in case,' she thought to herself, 'goodness knows what will happen next.'

The day of the school fashion show arrived. In the afternoon Kate helped to make posters for the wall and set tables ready for the evening refreshments. She was looking forward to the event and especially sharing something with her friend, Zelda. While Kate had been at school, James had spent his holiday with Zelda and both seemed to be very happy in each other's company. Kate hadn't seen Zelda very much but tonight Ben had promised James a game of badminton at the local sports hall while the ladies went to see the fashions. Kate was looking forward to a 'girl's night out.' As they handed in their tickets at the school hall entrance, Kate's Mum said that she could buy a new dress for the Christmas party. Zelda too fancied a new dress but she wasn't waiting until Christmas. While Kate chatted with her friends, Zelda quietly joined the models that were changing, in the staff room, behind the school stage. One of the mothers was panicking due to the absence of one of the models. Zelda took her chance.

'Don't worry. If she's late I'll take her place until she arrives,' offered Zelda.

The mother breathed a sigh of relief and pointed to a rack of clothes in the room.

'Fourth along, navy dress and you're the sixth one on,' she said.

Zelda made straight for the navy dress with white spots. It wasn't quite the right size, a little tight round the waist and rather short in length, but Zelda was wearing it and ready to model it on stage within three minutes. Her debut as a real fashion model was about to begin!

The proceedings began and Kate, sitting in the audience, was wondering where Zelda was. She didn't have to wait long. Model number six was announced and a witch, minus her purple dress, black hat and cloak, gracefully glided on to centre stage. Kate had to admit that her friend looked every bit a model and carried off the polka dot dress perfectly.

'Perhaps she would make a model after all,' thought Kate.

Zelda had observed the other models beforehand and smiled at the audience, giving twirls at just the right moment. The lady introducing each item moved closer to the microphone.

'Our model here is wearing a beautiful navy, silk dress with white spots, suitable for day or evening wear. As she walks along the catwalk you will notice the lovely swing of the skirt and new length which is very flattering to the figure.'

It was here that Zelda's attention was aroused.

'Catwalk?' she thought. 'Not much of a catwalk. Perhaps I can improve it a little.'

Within seconds cats appeared from everywhere. Black ones, grey ones, sleek and furry ones, Manx cats, Persians and Siamese. They clung to the curtains, climbed on people's laps and played with wires and cables from the lighting equipment.

'Oh no!' whispered Kate. 'She's done it again!'

Claudia, who had gloated as she waited for her turn to do her party piece, walked on to the catwalk just as a rather large, ginger tom cat decided to dash across from one side of the stage to the other. Over Claudia went, catching her heel in the hem of her dress and screaming and crying out at the sudden loss of her dignity. Her big moment as a star model had crumbled. She glared around her looking for someone to blame. Kate couldn't help laughing. This certainly was a show in a million. Zelda was puzzled as she watched people dashing everywhere, causing havoc and knocking over chairs and tables as they fought to be first leaving the hall. She looked questioningly at Kate as if to say, 'Why are they going?' Kate shook her head in dismay. Miss Selkirk, the headmistress, looked over in their direction.

She obviously realised, by the expression on her face, that Zelda and Kate had something to do with ruining the evening. She walked towards them.

'This wouldn't have something to do with your friend by any chance? I understand that she took you home on a broomstick the other day. Calling the neighbourhood cats in to join our fashion show must be another of her favourite tricks,' added Miss Selkirk.

Kate apologised and tried to explain that Zelda had meant well and had only wanted to help. Miss Selkirk suggested that she take Zelda home and make sure that she did not set foot in school again. Kate cringed. Now it didn't seem so funny after all. Kate was in trouble and Zelda was in disgrace! Zelda herself tried to excuse the evening's performance.

'I can't do spells very well when I'm over excited. I thought it actually went quite well, considering... How did I know that a catwalk has nothing to do with cats?'

'It seems to me,' added Kate, 'that you can't do spells very well at all. They are just not worth it so why don't you just forget about them altogether? Why didn't you just enjoy the evening like everyone else?'

'Because I'm not like everyone else!' cried Zelda. 'I'm not like you and I'm not a good witch. I cannot model and I cannot make spells. I can't do anything!' Zelda instantly turned a pale shade of orange and disappeared before Kate's very eyes.

'That,' said Kate's mum, 'was one very upset witch.'

Chapter 10

When Kate and her mum arrived home Ben and James were wondering where Zelda had gone. They retold the tale but could give no answers to their witch's whereabouts. James looked concerned but Kate reassured him that a witch could look after herself very nicely and would come to no harm. Later in the evening, as Kate pulled the duvet over herself and snuggled into her warm bed, she too, felt a little concerned about her friend's disappearance. She also wondered where the cats had got to as they had vanished as quickly as they had appeared. She wondered a lot about many things that night and eventually her imagination began to run away with her. She checked her thoughts just in time.

'Stop it my girl. Zelda will be okay. That's what comes of keeping company with a witch!'

She looked over to the house hole. All seemed very quiet. No sign of the mouse and no sign of a witch either. Kate lay on the pillow trying to figure out where her friend may have gone. She was already missing her, dreadfully, as she fell into a deep slumber.

The next morning Kate rose early and once breakfast was over and she was ready, she walked slowly to school. In fact, everything felt so uneventful that Kate had a strong fear that perhaps she might never see Zelda again. At school no one mentioned Zelda and nobody mentioned the fashion show. It was a whole week before Kate saw James to ask about Zelda and it was a very disappointed young man who had hoped to glean some information about a certain witch from his young cousin. No one had seen her and no one knew where to look. Kate sighed.

'I think she's gone home, back to where she belonged. She never even said goodbye.'

Life had returned to normal so quickly that Kate even wondered if she had imagined the whole thing. Perhaps she would have continued to think this had she not had a visit from James one evening after school. He was all excited and bursting to tell Kate his news.

'I'm going away, just for a while, but I want you to keep it a secret. I'm telling you 'cos you're my favourite cousin, and you love Zelda like I do, and - just in case something goes wrong.'

Kate frowned. 'What do you mean, goes wrong?'

James handed her a note scribbled on a length of purple ribbon.

'I found this tied to my gate. It's from Zelda, it must be!'

Kate read the words, which had been hurriedly written along the ribbon's length.

'Please come quickly. They won't let me come back. I need you to release me from this prison - tell Kate I miss her and sorry for leaving in such a temper. Say hello to the mouse for me. The mouse will ...'

At this point the note trailed away, leaving them questioning what the mouse would do.

'But where do you go? How do you get there?' queried Kate. 'We have no clues.'

'No,' added James. 'We must find some.'

Chapter 11

The first question James asked Kate was 'Where did you first meet Zelda?'

'It was my bedroom and Halloween,' answered Kate. 'She came to me on a broomstick - I opened the window - she helped me to save the mouse.'

'The mouse! Quickly, let's find the mouse,' shouted James excitedly as he ran towards Kate's room. 'Zelda writes "Say hello to the mouse; that's the clue!'

'Well, he's somewhere in there,' said Kate pointing to the house hole. 'You'd better say hello.'

'Where?' asked James.' 'I can't see a mouse hole.'

Kate suddenly remembered. 'It's invisible.'

James could see by Kate's expression that she was not convinced. However, he was not to be daunted. He knelt down at the place where Kate pointed and whispered 'hello' in an urgent gasp. To Kate's surprise a set of whiskers twitching with excitement appeared in the gap in her skirting board. The small creature looked up at James, winked a bright, knowing eye, and returned to its hole.

Within a few seconds the mouse was pushing what appeared to be a long handle towards the entrance. James pulled.

'A broomstick, it's Zelda's broomstick!' exclaimed Kate as James pulled the whole thing through the hole and into the bedroom.

'Zelda must have hidden it there for safety,' concluded James. 'Kate, open the window,' ordered James.

'You're not going to try to fly that are you?' asked Kate in horror.

'How else can I get to lands where witches dwell, except by broomstick,' remarked James positively. 'Zelda is our friend. We must trust her and her broomstick.'

Kate drew back the curtains, just as she had done on that eventful Halloween night, and opened the window wide. Then, she had done it to save a mouse, now it seemed she was about to save a witch.

'Do you think Zelda is in danger?' asked Kate. James looked pensive.

'No, I don't think so. Not in danger but maybe unhappy and needing our help.'

James laid the broomstick outside the window where it stayed magically suspended in mid-air while James climbed on to it. Kate was full of admiration for her cousin. The mouse sat on the windowsill looking on and he too, it seemed to Kate, was very impressed with James' heroic ride into the unknown.

'Wish me luck,' called James as the broomstick suddenly turned and zoomed forward into the darkness.

'Good luck,' whispered Kate but the mouse was the only one left to hear her say it and to see her fingers crossed very tightly behind her back.

Late into the night the mouse had returned to his house hole and Kate was lying in bed unable to sleep. After all it wasn't every day that a broomstick whisks your favourite cousin away into the night air to help a real witch. Kate missed Zelda and worried about James. She imagined all sorts of things happening to her dear cousin.

'Perhaps they don't like him and they've boiled him up in a cauldron,' she thought to herself. 'Or perhaps they are keeping him in a cage and feeding him lots of goodies to fatten him up for the oven.' Kate reassured herself that Zelda wouldn't allow such things to happen. 'I've been reading too many fairy stories,' she said to herself, more than once. Each evening Kate positioned her bed in front of the window. She sat looking out, searching for a glimpse of a broomstick returning home and each evening, the mouse would sit on the window sill, watching and waiting for the very same thing to happen. Kate made it a habit to bring a tasty piece of chocolate for her companion to eat while they sat together in the moonlight. The hardest part for Kate was that she did not know what was happening but she trusted Zelda and she had every faith in James. She would have liked to go with him but she knew James would never have allowed it. She also knew deep down that she had to be patient and just wait. Waiting and hoping can be very tiring, and so it was, each evening, Kate would fall asleep from straining her eyes, searching into the blackness.

The night James and Zelda returned, they were greeted by Kate, lying exhausted across her pillow with a little mouse curled up beside her. Their nightly vigil was over. James and Zelda were back and had such a tale to tell Kate in the morning.

Chapter 12

When Kate woke, Zelda was sitting in the armchair in Kate's room. Kate was bleary eyed and sleepy when she woke but she managed to find enough energy to jump out of bed and fling her arms around her long lost friend.

'I'm so pleased to see you. Is James OK?'

'Yes, I'm fine,' said James, grinning from ear to ear. He was carrying Kate's breakfast to her, on a tray. 'Room service, as usual.'

Kate climbed back into bed and in between cornflakes, boiled egg and buttered toast announced that she was ready to hear their story.

'You'll never guess,' said Zelda. 'Miss Selkirk is an old friend of Granny's. Granny says that her friend, Mildred Selkirk, was just like me when she was young, a bit of a rebel and a terrible witch. I told her about the fashion show but she knew already. Miss Selkirk, that is, Mildred, has been keeping an eye on me.'

'Wow. Who would have thought it? Miss Selkirk, a witch! What did they say about James coming to find you?'

'Well,' laughed James, interrupting. 'When I first alighted from my broomstick, not the most impressive way to arrive I may add, I found Zelda locked up in a tall, stone tower in a clearing in the forest. I saw her through an open window. I called to her. 'Don't worry. I will save you from this awful fate. Or words to that effect.'

'He looked every bit the knight in shining armour,' interrupted Zelda. 'He'd come to save a damsel in distress so I played along with him.' James blushed a little and rolled his eyes with embarrassment.

'You can imagine how I felt. I was right in the middle of a fairy story. Remember Kate? You always said she reminded you of Rapunzel. Now, here she was, locked up in a high, stone prison and there I was, on the ground, holding nothing but a broomstick.' Kate laughed.

'That's almost how the story goes. I wish I'd been there with a camera. Don't tell me you asked her to let down her hair,' added Kate with a grin.

'Yes, well almost,' answered Zelda. 'He asked for a ladder first. I didn't have one so he asked me to try to conjure up a spell to make my hair grow longer and strong enough to take his weight.' Knowing how Zelda's spells usually worked out Kate couldn't believe that her witch friend had managed that one.

'I didn't, but Granny did. Granny was in the tower with me!'

'So you climbed up Zelda's hair?' questioned Kate. 'Bravo!'

'That's exactly what Granny said,' explained Zelda. When James arrived through the open window, there was Granny. Granny clapped her hands approvingly, shouting 'Wonderful! Splendid!'

'James' face was a picture!'

'So why were you in the tower?' asked Kate.

'It was a test of courage and loyalty,' explained Zelda. 'Granny loves to put people to the test. She decided that if I wanted to swap a witch's world for your world then someone would have to help me prove that it was really worth it.'

'So did James pass the test?' asked Kate.

'With flying colours,' announced James proudly.

'Granny loved him,' added Zelda. 'He gave her some wonderful medicine.'

'For the cats?' asked Kate.

'Well,' said Zelda. 'It was meant for the cats but Granny tried it first, just to be sure. It did wonders for her arthritis so she's ordered lots more. Bainbridge liked him too and Granny approved of that. That's when she said I'd make a terrible witch so I may as well be a vet's wife.'

'A what?' gasped Kate in surprise!

Chapter 13

By the time the day of the wedding arrived Kate had decided that her cousin marrying a witch wasn't so bad after all. The newspaper people were there because they had heard that the whole wedding was going to be fancy dress following the theme of witches. The fact that James was marrying a 'real' witch was kept firmly under wraps. Kate was bridesmaid but instead of carrying the traditional posy of flowers she carried a red velvet cushion on which sat the guest of honour, a small, brown, furry mouse with ears erect and whiskers twitching. After all, if it hadn't been for the mouse…

The service went well. There wasn't a dry eye in the church as James and Zelda each answered 'I do.' Once married, and the register signed, James, starry eyed, led his bride outside to waiting photographers. The cars hadn't turned up for the reception but there was no need to worry. Everyone was very impressed when the bride, groom, bridesmaid carrying a mouse on velvet cushion and all the guests, climbed aboard the witches' broomsticks and zoomed off to the reception.

'Well. I never. They can do such wonders with technology these days,' muttered an old lady who was sitting outside enjoying the spectacle.

'I've never been to a wedding like it,' thought Kate.

At the reception she looked around the gathering of people. To one side of her was her mum, dad, Ben, aunties, uncles, and cousins, and of course Jack wearing his Halloween mask. To the other side sat a crowd of real, live witches! Zelda's granny and Miss Mildred Selkirk were sitting together, chatting, non-stop.

'They obviously have a lot to catch up on,' thought Kate.

There were witches of every kind. Tall ones, skinny ones, some with missing teeth, crooked chins and the prettiest witch of all, the bride herself. The mouse was eating crumbs from the table. Kate looked at James. Her favourite cousin had never looked so happy.

She turned and caught Zelda's eye. Her friend displayed a big, cheesy grin, and gave Kate a great big wink. Everything was strange and wonderful yet Kate couldn't help thinking that maybe, in fact, probably, this was only just the beginning...